piccolo

¼14

OCT   2015

violin

synthesizer

bassoon

cello

tuba

guitar

drums

banjo

cornet

flute

tambourine

lute

harp

ukulele

oboe

lyre

maracas

trombone

saxophone

mandolin

organ

bell

castanets

contrabassoon

xylophone

A

Is for Alliguitar

A

Is for Alliguitar

Musical Alphabeasts

BY NANCY RAINES DAY

ART BY HERB LEONHARD

PELICAN PUBLISHING COMPANY
Gretna 2012

For Sue, bluegrass fiddler
and sister extraordinaire
—N.R.D.

Copyright © 2012
By Nancy Raines Day

Art copyright © 2012
By Herb Leonhard
All rights reserved

Designed by Pinafore Press

ISBN: 9781455615575
E-book ISBN: 9781455615582

Printed in Singapore
Published by Pelican Publishing Company, Inc.
1000 Burmaster Street, Gretna, Louisiana 70053

Animals, instruments,
swing all around,
Mix – one for each letter –
now how do they sound?

A

is for alliguitar,
who has his
own picks.

B

is for banjaguar, who plays some hot licks.

C is for contrababoon, with sounds low and mellow.

D is for drumonkey, a loud-beating fellow.

E is for emuke,
who plays at luaus.

F is French hornet, who bothers the cows.

G is for **gorillute,** who soothes savage beasts.

H

is harpoodle, who
plays for fine feasts.

I is ibisynthesizer, a wizard with keys.

J is for jackalyre,
who sings
behind trees.

K

is for kangaflute. She toots while she hops.

**L** is for llamaracas –
for rhythm, they're tops.

M is for mandolion, who strums with his claws.

N

is newtuba,
who blares
without pause.

O is for organutan,
a talented guy.

P

is for pigolo,
squeaky and
high.

 is for queen bell,
buzzing while ringing.

R is for rhinoboe. His music is swinging!

S

is for saxofox,
with velvet-toned
tail.

is for tromboa,
who really can
wail.

U is for urchello,
mellow, with spikes.

V is for violynx,
who'll play
what she likes.

is for
wolbourines,
rhythm's their
game.

Y is for
yakastanets'
click-ty-clicks.

Z is for zebrass, getting their kicks.

When they all play at once,
every beast, bug, and bird,

They make music together
like you've never heard.